THE BEST WORST DAY EVER

Copyright © 2023 by Mark Batterson and Summer Batterson

Published in the United States by Multnomah, an imprint of Random House, a division of Penguin Random House LLC.

MULTNOMAH® and its mountain colophon are registered trademarks of Penguin Random House LLC.

ISBN 978-0-525-65389-9
Ebook ISBN 978-0-525-65390-5

The Library of Congress catalog record is available at https://lccn.loc.gov/2021056448.

Printed in China

waterbrookmultnomah.com

10 9 8 7 6 5 4 3 2 1

First Edition

Book and cover design by Annalisa Sheldahl
Cover and interior illustrations by Benedetta Capriotti

SPECIAL SALES Most Multnomah books are available at special quantity discounts when purchased in bulk by corporations, organizations, and special-interest groups. Custom imprinting or excerpting can also be done to fit special needs.
For information, please email specialmarketscms@penguinrandomhouse.com.

The BEST Worst Day Ever

written by
MARK BATTERSON and
SUMMER BATTERSON DAILEY

illustrated by
BENEDETTA CAPRIOTTI

·SHOES·

MULTNOMAH

Bert slid out of bed, a little sleepy-eyed.
Some days, waking up is hard to do.
That's when he stepped on his toy triceratops. *Ouch!*
Bert could tell, this was going to be one of **THOSE** days.

His favorite shirt was in the wash, so he had to wear his *second* favorite.

His sister was in the bathroom for a really long time.

His cereal got soggy while he took out the trash.

And then Noodles had chewed a hole in his sneakers, the fast ones.

What *else* could go wrong?

Then Bert remembered.

His mom was taking his sister to a gymnastics meet. And his dad had to work all day—on a Saturday! Instead of playing with his friends, Bert had to help his dad at the flower shop.

As Bert sat in the back seat, wishing this day were already over, the car hit a speed bump.

His juice box spilled all over his shirt. Now it was his *third* favorite!

Bert kicked his feet in frustration, but he didn't feel better. "Ugh," he said. "This day couldn't get any **WORSE**."

"Those are **BIG** feelings, Bert," his dad said. "Take a deep breath."
"A bad day doesn't have to end that way." His dad winked.

Bert took a big breath and let out a *sigh*, but he felt only a little bit better.

He looked out the window at all the other kids, who were flying kites, playing catch, and riding skateboards. *It looks like everyone else is having a fun day*, Bert thought.

When they got to the shop,
Bert dropped a vase full of flowers.

Everyone stopped and stared.
Someone even laughed out loud.

"This is the **WORST**
day ever!" Bert said to himself.

He snuck behind the counter. That's where he hid when he felt sad or a little bit mad.

"Give me five minutes," he heard his dad say.

Then Bert felt a tap on the top of his head. His dad knelt down. "How about a walk around the block, little buddy?"

"Can we take Noodles?" Bert asked.

"You'd better believe it. Go grab the leash!"

As they walked out the door,
it started to rain.

Bert's dad looked up and laughed.
Then he said to the clouds,
"You can't ruin my day. No way!"

"Rain or shine, Bert. Rain or shine!
Every day is what YOU make it."

Bert knew what came next.
His dad said it a lot.

"Win the day, Bert. That's all you can do!"

But Bert wasn't sure how.

His dad tilted his head, opened
his mouth, and caught a raindrop.
"Tastes awfully good," he said.
"See if you can catch one!"

"There are so many things we can't control.
Like nimbus clouds and not-nice people. But they
can't control us either, can they, Bert?" his dad
said with a grin. "**YOU** control you!"

"**Ten toes** and a **nose**. That's all it takes to turn things around, Bert! Wiggle your toes and smell the rain-fresh air!"

To Bert's delight, right there in the middle of the sidewalk, his dad took off his shoes, rolled up his pants, and jumped in a puddle.

Then he started singing. In the rain!

"Join me, Bert.
See if it helps."

And it did—quite a bit.

They rounded the corner and saw
a woman struggling to carry her bags.

"Do you know the best way to win
the day?" Bert's dad asked him.

"Make someone's day!"
Bert exclaimed.

"That's right. A helping hand can turn a frown upside down!"

Bert carried the woman's
groceries all the way to her car.

"Rain or shine," he told her,
"every day is what **YOU** make it."

"You made my day, young man," she said with a smile.

And that was the moment Bert felt almost all better!

"Look at the flowers. Look at the trees," his dad said. "They love the rain."

"So do dirty cars," Bert said with a giggle.

"So do kids who spill sticky apple juice," his dad said. "No bath tonight. You're already clean!"

"Look **up** and look **down**," his dad said. "Now look **all around**. If you're looking for something to be happy about, you'll always find it."

They turned the last corner
and walked into the shop.
They were wetter than water,
but Bert felt so much better!

He stood by the door the rest of the day, handing
out tulips and reminding everyone, "Every day is
what YOU make it." As he waved goodbye to each
customer, he exclaimed, "WIN the DAY!"

Finally Bert and his dad closed up
the shop with a turn of the key.

They hopped in the car
and headed home.

"What did you learn today?"
his dad asked with a wink.

"Rain or shine"—Bert winked back—
"a bad day doesn't have to end that
way! We can laugh at the clouds and
make someone **smile**."

After supper that night, his dad tucked
Bert in bed, all snug in the covers.

"Close your eyes, Bert, and count your blessings."

His dad tickled Bert's toes and kissed his nose.

"Ten toes and a nose. That's all it takes.
Every day is a gift, full of surprises!"

Bert let out a giggle.

"This was the **BEST** worst day ever!"